CW00392632

HANSEL

ANNALEE ADAMS

HANSEL

First edition. August 2022.

Copyright © 2022 Annalee Adams.

The moral rights of the author have been asserted.

Written by Annalee Adams.

This is a work of fiction. Similarities to real people, places, or events are entirely coincidental.

All rights reserved.

No part of this publication may be reproduced, transmitted or stored in a retrieval system in any form or by any other means, without prior written permission from the author, Annalee Adams. No part of this publication may be circulated in any form of binding or cover other than that in which it is published.

ISBN 97988 461 059 04

This book has been typeset in Garamond.

www.AnnaleeAdams.biz

To everyone,

Thank you for taking a chance on me.

I hope you love my books! ♥

ANNALEE ADAMS

GRETEL

A BLOOD-CHILLING SERIAL KILLER SHORT STORY

<u>Book One: Gretel.</u>

I became insane, with long
intervals of sanity.

Edgar Allen Poe

1

Swinging from the oak branch, old one-eyed Tallulah hung. How long she'd been there was anyone's guess. But I knew Mama had done it, it was in her nature. Tallulah was a mingy farm cat; we'd kept her around to keep the rat population at bay. There was far too many living in the tunnels under our home. Mama said Great Grandpa John had built the tunnels just before he died in the war; it was the perfect place to hide and keep the Devil at bay. I was born between the two great wars, never having the chance to meet him. But Mama said her Grandpa was a righteous man, a true family man. The problem was, that Mama believed it was too late, the Devil was already on Earth. She'd seen him in Daddy herself. Especially when

Daddy turned to Satan and drove the axe down on Jacob's head. Mama was never the same after that. Jacob neither. He was dead after all.

When I turned six Daddy was gone. I knew gone meant six feet under, digested by the worms and all manner of the insect kingdom. Daddy deserved it though. Jacob was innocent, playing on the porch when Daddy's temperature flared after he tripped over Jacobs's choo choo train, embedding the axe in his skull. Mama and Daddy had been arguing. She'd called him a man-whore and vowed to destroy the home wrecker that enticed him. We'd taken to praying hard back then. Mama made me pray every night before supper, twice before bed and once before the school bus came. We needed God's support over the next few years. The darkness had arrived, trying to corrupt us.

Sundays were the hardest day of the week, the day of rest and weekly appearances in the Red Room. I'd nicknamed it that after Mama told me of the blood spilt in the name of our lord. Church to me was a place of death and rebirth. A place where we could pay penance for our sins, cleanse our souls, and move on to a place of peace and love if only I knew how to love. Mama's method of paying penance was different to Father Georges. Mama used the iron to beat me every Sunday evening, crushing the Devil as she burned his wrath out of my body.

She changed after Daddy, becoming more possessive, with her eagle eye on me. She told me not to worry and said we'd be okay, we had each other. But I knew. Mama had a sickness that was eating at her brain. It made her do horrible things.

I remember when I was six, she huffed and puffed as she dragged poor Pete McArthur from down Old Saints Road. She wasn't very pleased with him, and when he started shouting, she decorated his body with kitchen knives and forks. Pete gurgled as she dragged him away. He did deserve to be decorated though, as Mama said he'd threatened to hurt us and take me away; she would never let that happen. That was the last I'd seen of poor Pete MacArthur.

It was dark back here, huddled in the cupboard, locked up with all manner of crucifixes and Bibles. Mama had kept me here for two days straight. She'd said the Devil had cast his eyes my way, after I bought little Joan Rayne home, from down on Phyllis Grove. I wasn't going to hurt her, I was curious. I was fifteen, she was six, maybe seven. She had been playing with her older sister Jane at the park as I'd rode past on my rusted old Raleigh bicycle. I'd stopped to see them, watch them as they weaved their way over the playground equipment. Joan was giggling, screaming for her sister to push harder, her frail body flying high, back, and forth. I didn't understand the reasoning behind it. Why would anyone want to hurtle through the air or round and round on a merry-go-round? There was no purpose to it. It looked like they were only experiencing mere fun, a relative concept I never quite understood. I could mimic many emotions, the good, the bad and the ugly; it was rare I ever *felt* them. But laughter when there was no purpose was an emotion I had always struggled to attain.

Dropping my bike, I wandered over and sat on the swing next to Joan. Jane grinned and attempted to push me too. She must have been only ten or eleven herself. I watched her, my face cold and unfathomable. Jane pushed harder, grunting as she shifted my weight off the ground. Her face flushed, matching the rash down one side of her cheek.

It was strange really, as I swung there my body began to lift, the lightness overtaking my brute nature. It was almost as though I could reach the Heavens the higher, I flew, perhaps this was how I'd meet God one day, and then that's when it happened. I reached out too far, slipped out of the seat, and crashed back down to Earth. In the moment after unconsciousness, I saw the sunlight bleach my eyes. Both girls ran over, and behind them stood an unearthly figure. A reigning God surrounded by love and light. Granted it could have been any passer-by, but to me, he had spoken. The words that left his mouth were not of our language. They were greater and more precise. For this God that stood above me, welcomed me into his arms and wiped away the emptiness I once felt. He showed me the beauty of the souls the girls both had. Then reminded me of the innocence a young child kept within them. To save them, I must destroy them. And to that I did; enticing both girls home that evening to meet my Mama.

2

Two days had passed. The only light I shared was through the line of sunlight that bled through the door frame. Mama hadn't fed me; only fluids were available to drink. The cupboard had a bucket, and a hole to the right side of the door where I could peer out and watch her bloody endeavours.

I'd brought the girls home, knowing full well what Mama would do to them. Mama believed they were touched by the Devil, with their rose-red rashes. I'd spoken of my connection to God. She believed it to be tricks brought on by the Devil himself. There was nothing I could say to make her see the truth and the brightness of their souls.

That's when she grabbed the fireplace poker, slamming Jane over the head, and knocking her unconscious. Little Joan tried to run, but Mama was on top of her in an instant. I tried to stop her. Tried to make her believe that I needed to destroy them, not her; they were mine to deliver into the light. God had passed the joy of cleansing their souls, to me. Instead, Mama slapped me across the back of my legs. My scrawny body flung across the room, and I slammed head-first onto the hearth. As I battled the fourth-coming unconsciousness, I saw Mama raise the poker high. Little Joan Rayne screamed as Mama slammed the poker down, skewering her from head to toe. I remember thinking how funny she looked with the handle of a poker sticking out of her mouth, her eyes bulged, face pale as snow; even her rose-red rash had pink in colour.

Now you could say I was guessing at how many days had passed, but considering I'd heard the letterbox open only twice, it would indicate it was two days. Although, I couldn't account for the time I had spent unconscious. So, I guess it was only an assumption; using the collective information I'd gathered.

I sat back and took a deep breath. The scent of my Mama's freshly baked meat pie wafted into the under stairs cupboard. Mmm. Now that's one dish that could bring me joy. Joy to my stomach as it digested the natural goodness Little Joan had to offer. I should have seen this coming. Mama said I was becoming too big for my boots. But I couldn't help it. I just kept growing.

Peering through the hole in the door I couldn't see any sign of the girls. The house was back to ship shape again and there was not an inkling that anything had even taken place. Plus no one would ever expect my Mama. She was the charitable pillar of this community; literally, she was the treasurer for the Church.

I sighed, thinking about Joan Rayne's delicate little body. I knew a girl like her once; someone so frail. I was only eight years old at the time, and I had made my first real friend; a pale little girl I'd grown to love. I remember the sun shining over the hilltop as the summers evening came to an end. We'd been playing on the street up by the woods when Mama came to find me. We were both young back then, and I didn't know any better. I tried to stop her. But no matter how hard I tried I could not convince Mama that we were just friends. She'd walked up the hill, down into the woods and saw us picnicking by the Hollow. We were laid down, soaking in the rays as Mama's shadow appeared over us. I wouldn't have minded, but at that precise moment in time, I had reached out and taken my friend's hand. Her delicate fingers cradled mine, skin so soft and smooth. We had turned to look at one another, long and dreamy into each other's eyes. For the first time in forever, she made me feel something, made me tingle inside, wanting and needing to be closer. Then Mama appeared.

Mama never liked my friend's family and the reputation they held. Her family were in cahoots with the mayor. A despicable, destructive mayor; and politics went against everything God had planned for us.

Mayor Jenkins was an old, harshly-spoken decrepit man. He was past his sell-by date and Mama believed he had earned his position by bargaining with the Dark One. Throughout my life, and on this very occasion; Mama showed me how to cleanse the souls of the taken. Taking their bodies and purifying them beyond a shadow of a doubt. When we were done with the mayor, he was free to walk the world of the righteous. His soul was blessed, his body destroyed, heartless and buried in the crypt alongside his wife and daughter.

Then it came to the picnic, our hands clasped, holding tight. She jumped up and hid behind me. Mama's big weighty body looked down on us, her face reddened, spittle foaming on her lips. "RUN!" I'd yelled, but her legs were too short. Mama outran her by a mile. She grabbed her long beautiful brown hair, yanked her backwards and pushed her frail little body down to the floor. Mama's eyes had turned to the darkness. She saw no good in her, nor her family, and I knew what that meant.

I'd pleaded with her and begged her to let my friend go. But no matter how hard I tried; I couldn't get Mama to release her hands from her neck. It was then I'd heard it, that horrific moment where the world surrounding us, was silenced, and all I could hear was the childlike screams of her gurgled voice, the voice that ended with the snap of her neck.

That was the first time I had seen Mama strangle someone, usually she played with knives, or whatever sharp implements she could mould into a weapon. Mama had always cleansed souls, but I'd never actually witnessed the death of another; especially not the death of a girl I liked.

Mama sat up, shifting her heavy weight from

my broken friend. Her mouth was wide, her face captured in the expression that ended with her life. My heart was broken.

3

Biting my lip, I had stepped forward, kneeling beside her. Her face flushed a purple-redness that began to dissipate. Pale freckles stood out as I moved my hand up to touch her rapidly cooling arm. The heat was dispersing, moving away from her peripherals, and conserving its energy for the torso. The problem was her heart didn't beat anymore; her body was limp and lifeless. Blue eyes began to glaze over, losing their shine; and with that, their colour. Silvered and soulless they looked up at the world. I remember wondering what her last memory would be, would it be the trauma of her last moments or the kindness of her connection to me?

Whispering thoughts filtered through my mind; would she remember me in Heaven? Would God take her soul and nurture her like a mother should to a child? Perhaps she would be better there, without me. Mama said we had cleansed her soul. She would live in God's hands, saved from the Devil's embrace. I knew she was right; my act of closeness had sealed the deal on her fate. We were too young, and unmarried. The thoughts I'd had, the feelings I'd felt, they should not have happened, and I was wicked for being that way. Her girlish innocence had my body stirring all kinds of illustrious emotions.

I helped purify my friend that day. Taking her heart so she lived beside me, loving me. Normally Mama would make a meat pie from the body. It wasn't right to waste a good meal. After all, we're big chickens walking around, and that's exactly what people tasted like, chicken, except chewier; especially when you got to the thighs, that meat is thicker, harder; but there's always a lot of it.

We had joints for a week after Daddy disappeared, I always wondered what he tasted like, maybe I knew; especially as Mama made a delight of a pie that evening. Supper was scrumptious with Daddy there to join us, feeding us.

Mama said we should bury her; she was my first love, and I needed a place to sit and talk to her. We buried her by the tree we had laid against. A place I often visited throughout my life. A place where I could share my devious thoughts without my Mama hearing or the Lord conversing.

The town had held a vigil for her, they'd pleaded for her return. Her mother spoke at the town fair, never a dry eye in sight. But still, some seven years later, she was never found. I remember the townsfolk gossiping, saying she had been taken away with the Circus. It had been in town back then, but it was never proven. The only proof they had was a vile photograph in Doug Bailstone's old air raid shelter. The Sheriff arrested him after an anonymous tip was given about the many girls he played with. Mama said Doug was a harbinger of death, hiding the evidence of his wandering hands through the over-active imaginations of silly little girls. Doug never made it to the courthouse back then. The bombs of world war twos Nazis turned him into a splattering of human matter over the corner of Anchorage Street. The case was closed after that.

The last few years of the Second World War were a blessing. We disguised the bodies as dismembered blast-worthy finds, and no one questioned how they died or why they were there. Mama had ended them; people who she deemed unworthy, those that needed saving. But I, I had to do the dirty work, chopping them up and burying them amongst the rubble. They were heartless corpses littering the bomb site. I kept each of them close, storing their hearts in my bedroom, under my bed. Mama never knew. She would think the Devil had touched me, corrupting my mind, body, and soul. I still hadn't taken a life yet. Mama did the gritty work. I enjoyed the bloody part, letting their crimson life slide over my hands, wrapping itself around me, smothering me, covering me in its rose-red goodness. I'd tasted it too, the bitter taste coating my tongue, making me cringe. Mama took the meaty bits and left me to burn or bury the rest of the corpse.

The floorboard creaked as a large figure covered the hole. Mama in her polka dot green swing dress and ruby red lipstick. She usually only dressed up for Church, she must have a date. Michael, the butcher from the next town had been around a few times. Perhaps she was meeting him again.

Scampering backwards I made it to the corner. This was the one person I never wanted to get on the wrong side of. The door flung open, and the face of a feisty woman glared at me. Her ragged hair was bustled up into a stiff bun, strands loose, soaked with sweat. She wiped her brow, her body creased, and she bent down, gripping my ankles with her thick, brutish hands, the hands of a killer. Pulling me out by my ankles, I yelped, my back dragged against the raw wooden floor; splinters threatening to embed in my skin.

"Time to clean up your mess Hansel," she boomed, letting go of my ankles. Spittle escaped her as she spat out the words "Get on with it!" I nodded, wincing at the pain.

"Okay Mama," I whimpered. "What would you like me to clean up?" I sat up. She bent down and slapped me across the side of the face.

"Those girls Hansel. They are your mess to clean up!"

I bit my lower lip. "What would you like me to do with them?"

"Finish off the living one. The older demon is paining me so. Her cries have erupted in my mind, and I cannot listen to the Devil's words anymore."

Jane… she's alive. I nodded. "Where is she?"

"Down in the tunnels. You need to end this

once and for all." She took a deep breath. "You know he can see you, don't you?"

"Who Mama?"

She growled, staring at me. "The Devil you insolent child!" I nodded. "He can see through the eyes of all his worshippers."

"Okay, Mama." She slapped me again. Harder this time. Tears welled in my eyes. "Don't you okay Mama me boy!" I nodded, standing up. I was taller than her now, but a lot less threatening. "Get down there and finish her off!"

I nodded and ran with my tail between my legs, heading out of the door to our underground tunnels.

4

I could recall these tunnels like the back of my hand. It helped that a siren song of cries drifted down the middle tunnel, enticing me closer still. These tunnels were built with wooden struts, something my Mama's grandpa thought would make them safer. They joined on to an old cavern about a mile in. I'd used the cavern as a way home after I'd snuck out for the night. I'd spent the evenings watching them, the people of Hilltop Meadows. Absorbing their nature, the way they held themselves, gestures they made. Even spoke out the words in different accents until I began to find myself in there somewhere. Mama found out though. She always knew the truth. After all, God was always watching.

The high-pitched wails of Jane Rayne echoed through the dank hallways, drawing me in. Turning the corner, I saw her raw, tragic face. A face etched in sorrow. Trauma encircling her veins. Beside her was the impaled body of her little sister Joan. A sweet six or seven-year-old, innocent and pure. Mama didn't realise. She didn't know any better. Knowledge wasn't at the forefront of her mind. In fact, I'd never seen Mama read a book besides the bible. How was she to know Joan's marked face was a medical marvel. Rosacea? To her, she saw the Devils hand handprint, and with faith on her side, she believed both Joan and Jane Rayne were there to entrap me with their devilish ways. Whereas really, they were both two young girls playing on a playground. Or were they? Perhaps Mama was right. Perhaps they did try to trap me with their whimsical ways? Isn't the Devil a master of mischief and a marvel of mystery? Doesn't he try to strike a bargain for your soul, promising you your greatest wish, then sending out the hell hounds to collect payment?

I sauntered over. Jane was sat against the stone wall tied up with ropes. I sat beside her, watching her dirty blond hair as she sat huddling her legs, face on her knees. Lifting my right hand, I felt it, fingertips tangling in her hair, brushing it back off her broken face. Dried blood encrusted her scalp. The remains of a strike from the fireplace poker.

Hiccups disguised as cries escaped her. Through the sobs and her heightened grief, she appeared distressed. Her body shook as the pain of her reality broke free. Jane was a mess, beyond recognition and pained by the very existence surrounding her. No matter how pure she appeared to be, this child beside me could not be saved. Perhaps Mama was right. Perhaps a swift death would free her broken heart and allow her to heal at the hands of God.

For if Jane were to stay in this world, she would succumb to the sacrilegious lessons taught to us. Jane would grow old, wither, and die. But die as one embraced by the Devil. This trauma had shaped her soul, made it vulnerable to the touch of the darkness, and no matter how hard I tried, there would be no saving Jane Rayne any longer.

I too had been touched by darkness. The Devil had welcomed me in and enchanted me back in sixth grade when I took a shine to Debbie Jackson. She was different, her skin mottled, breasts beginning to grow. She liked to play on the swings with me, outside of Montgomery High School. We'd stay after class and she'd roll up a cigarette, coughing and spluttering as she inhaled. She'd offer me some, but Mama had told me these girls were the Devil's playmates. Mama had said that if any girl was to offer me something evil, I must tell her in an instant. So, I did. Mama knew best. Debbie never came back to school after that, Quinn said her family had left in the night. Moved up North somewhere. It's supposed to be nice there.

I'd often sit on that swing, staring at the old cigarette butts on the ground, wondering about Debbie Jackson.

Jane would change. Her purity diminishes. She would turn into Debbie Jackson and be beyond saving. Over all this time, Mama was right. To let the pure live amongst the living was carnage in the making. They would lose their ability to shine. The Devil would seek them out and coil its body around there's, taking every inch of their innocence and corrupting it.

I looked down at Jane's frail figure. She used to be so vulnerable, innocent and godly. Mama's actions had changed her. I sighed. Perhaps Mama was only showing the depths of Jane Rayne's character. She would always turn into a monster, following the darkness. Clearly, that's what God meant when he spoke to me. Save them while I can. Bring them back to the light, and purify their bodies. So, I did.

Standing up I gripped the handle of the fireplace poker from little Joan's body. Yanking, it didn't move, instead, her body pulled towards me. Jane Rayne screamed for her sister, mouth agape, eyes wide. Every muscle shook, every tear wasted. For little Joan was dead, the cold corpse of a six, maybe seven-year-old. I walked over to her body. Silvered eyes, bloody blond hair. She used to appear pure, but even the Devil uses the innocent to entice the weak. I wasn't weak. I couldn't be, and I had to prove it.

I knew full well Mama was lighting a bonfire tonight, after all, it was Bonfire night, and a night of fireworks, toffee apples and s'mores. The problem was little Joan's body wouldn't burn well enough if there was a red-hot poker sticking out of it. I scratched my head, looking down at the lifeless child. Then again, surely it would be like a kebab, skewered on a fire. Shrugging, I left her be, after all, I didn't want to needlessly traumatise her older sister Jane any more than I had to. I knew I needed to end Jane's life. Then take a hatchet and chop her up into little pieces. But those eyes, those ocean blue eyes staring right back at me. Her bottom lip quivered, and she gripped her knees a little tighter.

Taking a long deep breath, I knelt, unclasped her hands from her knees and pulled her close. She needed someone to hold, to tell her it would be alright. So, she did. As she held me tight, I pulled the kitchen knife from my pocket, and hovered it over her back, positioning it where her heart would be.

"I'm sorry I have to do this Jane. But the lord has asked for you."

Pulling back, then pushing in, there was some resistance. The sound of it piercing her skin, sliced through me. She gasped, and cried out, holding me tighter. Her nails dug into my back; hot breath coated my neck. Panting, body rigid, she began to slowly slump into a pile. Letting her fall before my knees, I took her hand. Jane's eyes sparkled with tears, her rose-red face flushed, then paled. Lips parted; breathing slowed. Gripping my hand she quivered. "He's here," she whispered, a faint smile caressing her face. I gasped. Was she seeing what I saw? Could the lord truly be in our presence, saving her soul and taking her home to the promised land?

Nodding, I lay beside her. Her blood coated my shirt, her body began to cool, and as she took her last breath, I saw her chest fail to rise. A wave of shivers wrapped over my body, and her spirit left the tunnels, walking with God once more. I smiled. If tonight proved anything, it was that Jane Rayne had seen God, and I was his soldier, saving the innocent, returning them to sit by his side once again.

5

Sitting beside Jane's body, I smiled, really smiled. Her face delighted me, her silvered eyes stared back. With those eyes she had witnessed a miracle; my miracle, and I had given her that. I wonder what it would feel like to look through those eyes, to be Jane Rayne for that brief moment, feeling the grief of her sister, the joy of God's touch.

Holding her face, I did the one thing I had never done before. I sliced through her cooling skin, carefully removing it. She was beautiful, truly a wonderful young girl. If I stared through those eyeless sockets, I could feel what she felt; be human once again.

Taking her floppy face, I positioned it over my own. Sighing I could see she was too small for me. Perhaps an older girl would give me the ability to see what she sees and feel what she feels, and I yearned to experience that... I ached for it.

Even though her skin was tight, her nose too tiny; the feeling of her wet tissue against my face was soothing. Each lip became my own, we kissed inside as we met. Her lips parted as the gasping child she once was. Delicately licking her lips, my lips, I was able to taste her. A salty, bitter taste, one I wouldn't recommend, yet one that made my body stir. Rampant heat rushed through, and I twitched, enjoying the sensation. Licking her lips through my own, I tasted her essence. The blood of her body, the delight of everything that made her who she was. Seeing through her skin I sensed her beside me. Her heart is in my hand, blood spilling over me. Taking a deep breath, I exhaled. I finally felt joy. Felt the dance of life when I wore her face. I didn't act, mimic, or follow, this emotion was my own, and one I sought to enjoy once more. Sitting there I thought back, my lips curling, tongue licking her lips.

Continuing my life's journey, my thoughts turned to Barbara. I wondered what she'd taste like. Would her essence enter me like Janes had? I had become friends with Barbara in seventh grade. Mama was a chaperone at the disco, keeping her eagle eye on me all night. You see Mama looked normal. Her Church appearances and community bake sales all but sold her as the town's most charitable resident. Everyone knew her name. Everyone smiled and waved. My Mama was the best at blending in. She'd even had me fooled.

At the end of the disco, I slowly danced with Barbara Myers. She was a lonely little brunette with ash-blue eyes. I remember the swirl of hazel in her right eye as she stared deep into my own. Barbara was in my English class; she'd sit one behind me and two to the right of me. We'd often meet at lunch and sat alone talking through the mundane existence of our day. She was equally as clever as she was shy. But when she asked me to dance, I smiled and walked over to the dance floor. Taking her hand made me tingle. Her touch was so soft, her beauty understated. But I knew right then, when I looked over, Mama was watching, her eyes narrowed, her lips pressed tight. I couldn't let her be another victim, so I made my excuses and left the disco, heading home.

Mama never said anything later that evening. She seemed fine with the fact she'd caught me dancing with a girl. I left it at that, not wanting to rile her up and make her angry. She took to standing and showing me how to dance, ready for the next girl I wanted to ask. Perhaps she realised I was growing up, she must have, as she's never targeted Barbara through the years. Although Barbara said her family were big God lovers, she followed the righteous path, and perhaps that's why Mama didn't bat an eyelid.

Me and Barbara became best of friends. We

fled the fields together, climbed trees together and even swung on the swings, she loved the swings. That's when Quinn and Daventry joined us. A chaotic mix of four individuals from different backgrounds but the same upbringing, God.

Mama had accepted them all into our home, every one of their families living the righteous path to the promised land. Mama said I needed a good influence in my life, people who would steer me in the right direction. She'd said she couldn't be there all the time to protect me. I'd happily accepted. Agreed wholeheartedly to be good and keep my soul clean. But there was always that lingering feeling. The darkness settled under my skin. I'd find myself watching my friends, mainly Barbara. I enjoyed working out their mannerisms, their unearthed nature taking heat. They were my test subjects in an experimental world. I followed in their footsteps, laughed when they laughed, cried when they cried. Picking up on the cues of normality, I began to shine. It was hard though, to keep the facade from cracking at the seams. But it was necessary. Mama said we had to blend in, it was the only way to cover up our ways. If the Devil caught us, all would be over; God had to prevail. So, I listened and watched. I took in the high notes and the low, following their rhythm as I persevered through life.

Now the war was over, the disposal of bodies proved more difficult. I had taken to using the hatchet, chainsaws, and bin bags; keeping the best cuts for the freezer. The thing is, you have to prepare the body sooner than later, after three to four hours the muscles begin to stiffen, and after twelve hours it would be as stiff as a board, and a bugger to slice and dice. Plus, the meat was useless after a day, so little Joan Rayne was disposed of, and her meat wasted. I hated wasting a good body.

Finishing off I sealed the pieces of Jane's meat and put them in the freezer. Luckily, we had a large chest freezer, capable of storing several bodies.

Lighting the bonfire, little Joan became my very first kebab, granted not one I'd ever eat; old meat can make you sick, but still, the sizzling of the oils in the skin, and that barbeque smell captivated me. It was time for dinner, Mama's meat pie and roasted vegetables. I licked my lips, I hadn't eaten for quite some time, and any food right now would be a marvel.

Heading back into the house, the sun began to set, and we tucked into our meal, before heading out for the evening fireworks display.

6

So now I'm here, on Ninth Avenue with the flash bangs and devil bangers. It was the perfect night for a cover-up. Almost like when we cowered in the air raid shelters through the end of the war. We'd survived that, we were invincible.

Mama took this time to educate the lesser youths of this sleepy little town, and with the fireworks display screaming out before us, no one could hear their screams. Guy Fawkes had taken over with Fizzle Whizzlers and Shrilling Sedennas. The shrieks of her burning flesh never entered the minds of Barbara, Quinn, or Daventry. Not one of my friends knew the truth about little Joan Rayne. She'd been missing two days now, ever since All

Hallows' Eve when Mama took down the pitchfork and skewered her over the fireplace like a pig in a hog roast.

Mama always saw herself as the saviour of Hilltop Meadows, a messenger of God, doing his dirty work so he didn't have to.

The Rayne girls wouldn't be her last. I didn't mind though; she kept all the good girls for me. I turned fifteen last week. Born two days before the Devil entered our miserable little town. Two whole days for God to find me and purify me before Halloween came about and the darkness reigned our forgotten home.

Mama said I'd live long enough to hear the words of God himself, and she was right. He had come to me the day before yesterday; spoken in the true language of the ancient ones, yet somehow, I understood his riddled tone. Mama said he'd blessed me. Blessed me because of the faith I brought to this family. We were the only ones left after all. Daddy had gone six feet under, and little Jacob died at his hands, taken before his time. Jacob still lives with us though. His frail body was wrapped and preserved beside his twinkle toes teddy bear and Jimmy Lane Choo Choo train. He'd always loved those toys, not that he'd got much else to play with.

Mama had said we didn't need the mundane toys man gave us, for we were made of something greater, something more ethereal than mankind. We were made by God himself.

Jacob always sits there, eyes bled to mush over the years as his skeletal frame cowered beneath the Hessian wraps. I missed him though, even though he was there. I missed his voice, his laughter. Before his soul returned to the lord, he used to laugh; it was rare, but when he did the light in his eyes was blinding, like the sun setting one last time. He was purer than any of us could ever be. Too pure for this world perhaps.

That's how I see it anyway. There are some out there just like Jacob. Too innocent. Too unbroken. They will never last against Satan's sadism. Mama and I had made a pact after Jacob passed; we had agreed to save as many as we could along the way. That was our purpose, our belief in life; the more we saved, the brighter our afterlife would shine.

It was true too. I'd seen it when Mama had the priest dunk me under the water down at Old Billows Pond. Mama had said he was a priest. He certainly looked like one. But the way he'd held me under, the strength of his grip; he hadn't seemed very godly to me. Well, no matter how hard I think back, I can never remember seeing that priest again.

So back to Joan and Jane; two girls burnt to a cinder. The smell of fresh meat barbecued, cured of all evil that welled within their earthly bodies. I could breathe in the smoke in the air, feel their spirit worshipping my body from the inside out. It enticed me, curled around me. Their blond curls, pale fragile bodies. Each of the girls had looked up to me as their saviour, their eyes pleading against their rose-red faces. It was rare apparently to have two children with the rash in the family. But Mama said it was because their mother was a whore, she'd slept with the Devil when he walked the earth one Halloween all those years ago. I vaguely believed it. After all, their mother, Trisha Bates, was a curvaceous sinner. She'd used her womanly body to entice the preacher's brother, I'd seen it so. Plus, Daventry had said she saw Trisha Bates doing ungodly things in Mr Stevens's trousers behind the bike shed after class. Mr Stevens was our English teacher, he was married too, but the Devil never took the men in our town, only the women. So, Mama said we must encircle their souls with our devotion. She said, our lord would take their suffering, and cleanse their spirits, as we purified their bodies. I knew after the girls; that Trisha Bates was next on my mama's naughty list.

7

It was coming to the end of the night, and the three of us were sat on the embankment at the end of Farmers Lane, watching the fireworks display from afar. My house was close by. We owned the farm at the end of the street. It was a place passed down through our family, and exactly what we needed to live our lives, taking the lives of the sinners amongst us.

Barbara joined us, sitting beside me, she was fourteen now, but always looked so young, radiant, and beautiful; her skin the smoothest I'd ever seen.

Barbara sat snuggled into me, her head resting on my shoulder.

"Do you think it's nearly over?" she asked,

looking at her wristwatch.

I smiled, turning to face her. Her eyes glinted in the moonlight. "Yes. I believe so."

Barbara smiled and rested her head on my shoulder again.

Quinn looked over. "Hansel come join us!"

Daventry snickered, throwing a banger in my direction. Barbara pulled away, curling her arms around herself, I huffed, my eyes narrowed.

Why would he do that? He can see I'm happy where I am!

"Hansel!" Quinn shouted. I shook my head, hands curled into fists.

Taking a deep breath I peered at Barbara. She grinned, moving back up to me. "Ignore them, Hansel, it's you and I remember." I grinned and nodded. We sat there for a while, watching my friends' chaotic endeavours. Then Barbara's spindly legs began to shake, she pulled her arms tighter around them. Huddled in her coat she shuddered. "I must be going home."

I nodded, standing up just as she did. "I'll walk you home," I said. She smiled, and we waved goodbye to Quinn and Daventry.

"You're boring Hansel!" Daventry shouted after me. Quinn laughed and they continued throwing fireworks around.

Watching Barbara step down off the embankment, I paused. Her skin curved around her frame, her body slinking back into itself when she pulled her coat tighter. I stepped forward. Her brown hair whispered across her face as the wind swirled past us. Soft, smooth skin delicately cushioned her body, so tender and beautiful. She held out her hand. "Are you ready?"

As always, I took it. My fingerless gloves prevent our hands from entirely touching. But frozen fingers danced together as we clasped each other and walked on. "You don't have to walk me home every night."

I smiled. "I know. But I like to."

Barbara bit her bottom lip. I watched,

picturing the taste her tongue must be experiencing right now.

We walked past Eric Bannister's home, down past the dilapidated old mill and turned right onto Forks Lane. The third door is on the right. I could walk Barbara home blindfolded if I had to. I'd been walking this route for years now, ever since I met her. She would always wait by the front door until I turned and waved, walking away.

Barbara's mother was a strange one, she never had much time for her, always keeping her younger sister occupied, rarely giving me the time of day. Mama had said they were still grieving back then, they'd lost their father, her mother now a widow. Too much loss in one family can corrupt even the purest of souls. But Mama did her duty, taking homemade meat pies, and keeping them fed and watered.

After Jacob passed and Daddy disappeared, Barbara was there for me. I remember her mother bringing us homemade lasagne, pasta bake and soup for two weeks straight. Mama had been so grateful. She had lost her way for a while back then.

It wasn't until Mama used the axe from Daddy's study that she started to feel at peace again. She tracked down the homewrecker my Daddy had been having an affair with and ended her life that very evening. I remember it clearly, remember the cries of her little girl. The crimson blood as it exploded from her neck. The baby girl's wet hands as she slipped on her mother's remains in an attempt to escape my Mama's vengeance. The fear in her eyes as the blade cushioned her throat. It was unravelling to watch. Almost perfect to see. I can't quite put my finger on it. But after what that woman had taken from us, she deserved nothing less than what my Mama had dealt her and her beloved daughter. I only wish she had ended the girl first, made her watch, grieve, and see. Then maybe she would have seen a small portion of the pain she had caused my Mama.

Barbara let go of my hand. The softness of her touch escaped me. We had reached the front porch of her family home. "Thank you," she said, smiling sweetly.

I nodded, smiled, and wished her goodnight. "Hansel," she said.

Turning back, I looked at her. "Can we take a walk alone one day?"

I smiled. "Sure."

"By the cliffs perhaps. It's beautiful there." I nodded. "Okay," she smiled.

"But not tomorrow, Mama needs my help tomorrow."

"The day after?" I agreed, nodding. After saying our goodbyes, I turned and headed home to my Mama and the char-grilled remains of the Rayne girls.

The next morning Mama called me into the yard. We had chores to do, God's work. As I walked out, I saw one of the chickens squirming in her big hands.

"Here Hansel, your turn."

She shoved the chicken's head in my hand, wiping her hands on her dated floral dress. The chicken squirmed and wriggled. My grimy fingers held tight as my face paled with fright. She looked down at me, her dark hair covering her face.

"It's easy Hansel. You grab its neck, take the hatchet and pound it down on the dirty thing."

I nodded, biting my bottom lip.

She crossed her arms. "Here!" Mother held out the bloodied hatchet. I looked up and winced.

"Take it, Hansel! I haven't got all day!" I looked at the chicken, it was small, fragile, and scared. A sense of dread enveloped my body. I'd never killed a chicken before, Mama usually did it. It didn't seem right.

"Hansel do it! It will feed us! God needs us to do this!"

Shoving the hatchet in my hand she stood over me. I nodded, looking at the chicken in my hands. The fright in its eyes was transforming. I'd only ever killed to save souls. First, it was my mingy farm cat Tallulah, then one of the Rayne girls. But this chicken wasn't corrupted by the Devil, nor would it be. It was a living, breathing food source. The type of meaty bird I enjoyed, was succulent and smoked. Mama always added her version of herbs and spices, bringing out the juices to tantalise and corrupt your taste buds. Even if the fright in its eyes disturbed me, my hunger for meat overruled. I lifted the hatchet, the sharpened blade was coated in blood, not necessarily animal blood, quite possibly human, from a body that wore a skirt, swung on swings, living a carefree life.

Positioning the chicken's neck down on the ground, I took a deep breath and slammed the weighty hatchet down, missing my fingers by a mere inch. The chicken squawked, writhing, and wriggling in pain; its neck half attached to its body. My aim was off, catching the bird, rather than chopping its head off. I let go and yelped, dropping the hatchet. Mama laughed, shook her head and tutted. The chicken's body seized and squirmed, it looked at me with that all-telling fear.

Mama walked over, lifted her grubby barefoot, and with all her might, slammed her heavy body down on the poor bird's head. Brain oozed everywhere. Wiping her sole on the grass, she kicked the chicken's body aside, its corpse still twitching.

Part of me wanted to vomit. The other part was fascinated. The chicken's blood flowed free, its body still convulsing. Rays of light shone down through the clouds, highlighting his corpse, and bathing it in God's warmth. It delighted me how the body could recall its last movements through the memory of its muscles. Muscles, tissue, ligaments, and organs, are all there for the taking.

Picking up the hatchet, and the bird's corpse, Mama walked over to me. Bending down, she grabbed me by my ankle and dragged me kicking and screaming over the gritted dirt drive, burning my back, and banging my head over the stones and rubble. "Your turn," she said, slamming my head down on the butcher's block.

"Mama no!" I yelled. The force of her was unbearable. A thick brutish hand held me in place. The ratchet held high, dripping from the blood of its previous victims. Shit. Was she really going to do this? I fought back, kicked, clawed at her arm, anything, and everything to stop the inevitable.

Mama shrieked as my nails dug into her forearm. She slammed the hatchet down, missing my face, nicking my ear, and chopping off a handful of my hair. I fell backwards as she released me, falling onto the floor. She laughed, her whole body shaking.

Even at fifteen, and taller than her, I was still weak and feeble. Mama had been given God's body. She'd said her curves, her bosom was the work of the lord. It gave her strength to handle the tasks he gave us, and he gave us a lot.

"Finish it," she demanded, hurtling the chicken's body at me. Catching it, the blood and bile separated, covering my ripped tee shirt. I sighed, sniffled back my tears, wiped my eyes on my arm and dropped the body down on the butcher's block.

It had stopped moving now. Completely dead. Body cooling by the second. I wondered if the chicken had the better end of the deal, rising in God's warmth, sat beside him in the Church of all pure and sacred.

Wiping my forehead, beads of sweat and grime coated my arm. I sat down at the rickety kitchen table and began plucking the feathers from the cooling corpse before me. Each feather was unique, browns, oranges, and creams; you could make something spectacular out of these, perhaps something Barbara might like. I paused, placing the bloody feathers in a glass jar I found; then proceeded to stick my hand in and remove the entrails from the chicken's body. Half an hour later I'd cleaned up, wrapped the meat, and put it on a roasting tray, ready for dinner.

Taking a deep breath, I poured a glass of my Mama's homemade lemonade, winced at the bitter taste, and added two more spoonful's of sugar; much better!

"What's that banging and clattering?" Mama yelled, from the front room. "Have you finished with the bird?"

"Yes Mama," I replied, walking in to see her.

"Oh Lord, you need a bath, you're covered in blood and guts."

"I don't mind Mama!"

She walked over, slapped me across the face, and said, with spittle foaming at her lips, "I mind! Now do as you're told boy and have a bath!"

My hand raised to my red face, and I nodded. "Yes, Mama."

Feigning a smile, I walked out and headed over to the bathroom, running the water. It was lukewarm at best. A quick bath it is then! The clock on the wall chimed three in the afternoon. I smiled. Barbara would be here tomorrow morning; I'd promised her a walk by the cliffside.

Climbing over the edge of the bath, I got in. Immediately the water began to turn to a shade of pink. Blood from the fallen corpse coated the water with its essence. Blackened dirt scrubbed out of my hair, whiskers of stubble fell around me as I shaved, and when I was finished, I laid back in the dark bath and spent a few minutes thinking.

Her. Not Barbara, but my first kill; Jane Rayne. Closing my eyes, I could picture her; her tear-stained face, her quivering lips, and dry blood coating her perfect figure. She was so young before, so full of life. But none of that mattered, I knew it was either her, or me. Mama had already threatened me several times in the last week.

The noise it made as the knife pierced her skin, is one I shall never forget. I wonder if she'll remember me in Heaven. Will she thank me for taking away the pain of her life, and returning her to her one true father, our God? I hope she does, I hope when it's my turn, I see her and we can swing high again, rising through the Heavens. I smiled; I'd like that.

Finishing up, I dressed and joined Mama in the front room. She surprised me with a present, the first in many years, but a treat she rewarded me with after my first kill. The board game Scrabble was a relatively new game Mama had invested in to keep the boredom away. It wasn't easy, I wasn't the best at spelling, and often I thought my Mama was cheating, with words that only she seemed to come up with; not surprisingly, she won.

After cleaning up, having dinner and a creative discussion regarding my first kill, I went to bed. The day had been a long one, one where, although I loved my Mama, I would always tread carefully in her presence. Nursing a headache, my head hit the pillow and I soon fell fast asleep, dreaming of the one and only love of my life, Barbara Jane Livingston.

9

Eyes close, dreaming of the faint lavender scent Barbara wore. Her ashen skin was delicate and soft. Her smile, teeth so white they could blind you in the sunlight. Her composure, that of a young lady, is a classic timeless beauty. Everything about her enticed me, called out to me. She was my angel sent from God. A gift from the Heavens for the good work I had done in his name; and for that I am eternally grateful.

Taking a deep breath in, I breathed in the aroma of charcoal. An old reminiscence of the bonfire we had last night. Mama had two bodies worth of meat now. One skewered, cooked as a kebab, but sadly inedible, the other chopped up as joints, keeping us fed for several more weeks.

I'd sat down with Mama last night when she asked me what my first kill was like. I explained, although not in the great detail she perhaps wanted. But carefully, steadily describing the force of the blade, the squeal of Jane Rayne. Like a pig, she'd said, which I thought accurately described the noise. I know the human side of me should feel bad. I should feel some inkling of pain as I stabbed her in the heart. But I didn't. I couldn't; and from watching the world, I know that's not normal. Mama said God made me this way. Made us both this way. We had to be heartless to be able to bring his children back to him. It made sense, but I knew, somewhere deep down, it had to be wrong.

To be honest I was surprised the police hadn't dragged us in with silver cuffs by now. Locked up, key thrown away. But through his divine intervention, we always seemed to get away with it. It's the bonus of having a farm, or a creepy underground lair. The police didn't bother us, didn't care, and would rather hunt down drunks and pickpockets than concentrate on disappearances.

I slumped out of bed, stretched, yawned, and pulled on my clothes. The ones from yesterday would have been fine if I hadn't had chicken stew decorating them, raw chicken stew at that. I sighed, trudging to the bathroom, and washing the grime off my face.

Barbara was due round today; she'd promised to help me feed the chickens and catch up on Mama's chores. Mama would be happy if she pitched in and helped.

After breakfast, there was a knock at the door. Mama ignored it and went about making a pie for dinner. I turned around to see Barbara had let herself in. She stood in the hall, smiling away. I grinned and looked at Mama, who was still busying herself in the kitchen. Taking Barbara's hand, I whisked her upstairs to my bedroom, closing the door behind us.

It was the first time any girl had entered my room. I was excited to find out how far Barbara's friendship with me could go.

"Hi Hansel," she said, grinning. I smiled. "I like your room. It's very… white."

I laughed; she actually made me laugh! "Mama doesn't' like many colours, she says they occupy the mind too much."

Her eyes widened, she smirked and nodded. Damn. This girl was going to get me in all kinds of trouble!

Looking down at our hands, Barbara looked up and our eyes met. My body relaxed, taken in by the moment. Those bright blue eyes, the swirl of Hazel decorating one, arched around the pupil. Delicate, pale skin, so young, unaged. My hand reached out to stroke her cheek. The touch sparked something inside of me, stirred an emotion I had only once ever felt. She was my soulmate, and I knew she would be with me forevermore.

Stroking her face I sighed. Such a beauty. Is it wasted on a slender creature such as she? Would she love me forever, would she stay with me? Knowing what I am, the job I have to do? Will I lose her if she finds out? Surely God wouldn't have sent her to me if she would likely run from my purpose. It was at that moment I urged to show her. To share every part of myself. To believe I could be loved for who I am, what I must be.

I pulled away. "What's wrong?" she asked, her brow furrowed.

"I just…"

"It's okay Hansel, I won't bite."

I smiled, nodding. She turned to me, leaned forward, and kissed me on my cheek. The wetness of her touch left me shuddering with arousal. She laughed. A high-pitched squeal of a laugh.

"Shush!" I said, panicked. If Mama heard her, I knew exactly what she would do! I couldn't lose another one.

"It's fine Hansel. She won't hear me." She

grinned. I took a deep breath, pulled her close and kissed her. For a first kiss, it lasted longer than I ever thought it would. Lips cushioned against one another, the warmth of her body against mine. Tongues searching, delving deeper. We became one in that moment. A moment where I could feel what she felt, truly feel.

She pulled back, laughing. "Come on Hansel, haven't we got chickens to feed?"

My face reddened. I nodded, trying to kiss her again.

She stood up, lifting me to meet her. "I'm not the one you should kiss Hansel. There is another girl you need to find. The perfect girl. A special young girl that needs to be rescued."

"Rescued?"

She nodded. "I know what you do Hansel. I have always known."

My jaw dropped. "You know."

She smiled, pulled me close and whispered in my ear. "We do God's work Hansel, and there's much more for us to do."

My God, she was spectacular. Every inch of me stood frozen to the spot, encased by her whispers, taken back by her love. She too was a saviour, a messenger of God. We both were and for now… we had a job to do.

10

A day spent with Barbara was a pleasure indeed. Walking outside she commented on Tallulah. She was clearly a cat lover, I felt bad for what I had done. Passing me a knife, she helped me take her down and bury her. Mama walked out and saw us, she rolled her eyes, collected the chicken eggs, and walked back into the house, not saying a word.

After helping me with choirs, Barbara had promised to meet me the next day. Today. The night's sleep before had been a restless one. I needed to be close to her again, to kiss her lips, touch her skin, absorb her into myself. But when the morning sun rose, and a new day began, I often wondered what she meant when she said I had another girl to kiss, a perfect girl that needed saving. Perhaps there was one. Perhaps that was my destiny after all.

"Come on, let's take a walk," she said, walking into my bedroom. She'd snuck in through the front door, avoiding Mama's eagle eye, hiding here with me.

"Okay." I slumped off the bed, stretched, then washed and dressed in the bathroom. By the time I had finished, Barbara had made the bed and was sitting eagerly awaiting.

"Where do you want to go?" she asked.

"I believe I owe you a walk alone by the cliffside." It was one of my favourite places. She nodded and we took one another's hands, disappearing out the door and down the road towards White Hill Cliffs.

It was a bright and beautiful morning. The crisp leaves had rotted under the frosty breath of Winter, and the morning dew had settled on the fields, watering them, and helping them grow.

Nature was always something I admired, how it believed in itself, took over your surroundings and was triumphant, even in the darkest of spaces. No matter how bad the world got, nature would always push back and survive.

Walking with Barbara, holding hands she smiled at me. It was still early here, and a little chilly as I pulled my coat up tighter. I do wonder though, if she knows everything I do, does she truly agree, could she stomach the dark parts, killing the weak?

Smiling back, I noticed how pale her complexion looked against the cool exterior of the harsh winter scene around us. Was she cold? She wasn't shivering, so perhaps she was fine after all. Maybe she preferred winter. She gripped my hand tighter and sped up the walk until we reached the cliffside.

Looking over the edge she commented on how far down it was. Her eyes are wide, lips curled up at the corners. She was enjoying it, the danger, the adrenaline rush of being so close. I grinned. It would be so easy to let go of her hand, give her a little push, watch her eyes bulge, face retort into a scream as she fell. The sound of her crashing on the rocks, broken bones, bloody tissue, there wouldn't be anything left of her.

But then what would I do? I'd be alone in this world, with only my Mama to talk to. After all, Quinn and Daventry were a waste of my time, they acted like children with their amateur games and immature thoughts.

I pulled Barbara back from the edge. "Watch you don't fall!"

She smiled and allowed herself to be wrapped up in my arms. "Oh Hansel, are you worried about me?" I looked down to the ground. "That's so sweet." She laughed, pulling away. "Let's take a walk to the park, there's swings there, I bet you'll love the swings."

My brow furrowed. "How did she know?"

"What's wrong Hansel?" she asked, as we

started to walk.

I narrowed my lips. "Nothing."

"You do like swings, don't you?"

"Yes, but…"

"But what Hansel?"

"How did you know?"

She laughed. "You told me silly!"

I paused for a moment. Perhaps I did. Shrugging, I gripped her hand tighter, and we continued walking to the park.

At the park, a young girl was swinging high on the swings. She must have been only eleven. She reminded me of the dead Jane Rayne.

"Let's go and talk to her," Barbara said, pulling me over. "She looks like she needs a friend."

I smiled and let Barbara lead the way, pushing me forward.

Standing beside the swinging girl, she sauntered to a stop. "Hi," she said, looking up at me. Her eyes were the richest shade of green.

"Hi," I said, sheepishly.

Barbara laughed. "Tell her your name," she said, nudging me forward.

"I'm Hansel, what's your name?"

"I'm Lola-Jane," she said. "But my friends call me Lola."

"Can I call you Lola?" She nodded and smiled.

"Do you like swings?" she asked.

"Yes. Yes, I do."

"Then jump on Hansel, I'll push you."

I turned to see Barbara sitting down on the bench behind us. She smiled and waved, urging me forward.

I nodded, sitting down on the swing.

Lola yanked me backwards and huffed as she pushed me forward. "Don't fall off!" she said. Then proceeded to tell me how to swing faster. Legs in, legs out. Legs in, legs out. The rhythm of the movement catapulted me forward, higher, and higher. She squealed and clapped, jumping on the swing beside me. "Let's see who can swing the highest!"

I laughed. She made me laugh!

I turned to see Barbara had gone, perhaps she needed to go home for dinner, time was getting on after all.

Slowing down, I smiled. She slowed down beside me. "I have to go," I said.

"Where?"

"Home, I live on the old farm near Billows Pond." She nodded.

"Okay, but I'll be here tomorrow if you want to swing some more."

"I'd like that, Lola." I smiled. "See you tomorrow!" and with that I left the park, smiling all the way home.

11

The next day I was excited to see Lola again. Running down I checked the kitchen and Mama was nowhere to be seen. Phew! She would know something was going on.

Grabbing a home-baked muffin, I put on my boots and left the house. The door creaked when I closed it. Mama was walking up the dirt drive with chicken feed in her hands.

"Hansel, where were you? You're meant to feed the chickens!"

My face paled. "Sorry Mama, I overslept."

"Overslept! Don't you think I want to oversleep?"

My head lowered to the floor.

"Look at me Hansel," she yelled. "Have some

respect!"

I looked up, quivering in my boots. "Sorry Mama!"

Dropping the chicken feed, she stomped over, red-faced, hands fisted. I winced, backing off towards the house.

Thick brutish hands grabbed me by my ear, and I yelped. She dragged me inside. "Don't you think I deserve a break, Hansel! All I ever do is clean up after you!"

"I'm sorry Mama!" I cried, salty tears cushioning my lips. "It won't happen again!"

"No, it damned well won't when I peel your eyelids off!" she growled, spittle foaming at her mouth. "You try and sleep then!"

My jaw dropped, she slammed my head down on the butcher's block, picked up a knife and crushed my face into the blood-stained wood. "No Mama! No!" I yelled, pleading with her.

Taking the knife she shifted her weight forwards, crushing me more. I grabbed at her arm, batting it away, screaming at her to let me go!

Holding the blade over my eyes she pushed forward, the tip almost touching my eyelids. I blinked repeatedly, batting away her arm. "Stop moving you, insolent child!"

"No Mama!"

My eyelashes feathered against the sharpened blade; lids open wide to stop her. I cried and cried, the images blurring before me. Leaning down her tongue positioned on her bottom lip. She was concentrating. She was going to do this!

Horrified I pulled away with all my might and hit her arm really hard, and as the knife dug in, it sliced my cheek from the corner of my eye down to my lips.

Yelping I fell to the floor. Mama fell forward, the knife slicing her other hand, she cried out.

Blood misted my face, running away from me.

Picking myself up I turned to face my Mama, her knife still in hand. She was holding her other hand up while grinning. "That's my boy!" she cried, laughing.

"What?" I asked, broken, and confused.

"I was waiting for you to grow some balls!"

I stepped back as she waved the knife around while talking. "I, I don't understand Mama!"

"You've taken the next step, Hansel. You can fight for yourself now!" She grinned some more. "I knew this day would come!"

"What do you mean?"

"Come here," she said, pulling me into the front room.

We stood before the mirror above the fireplace. "Look!"

I was covered in blood. It ran down my face, dripping on the wooden floor. "You cut me!" was all I could say.

"But you cut me, Hansel," she said. "You stood up for yourself, finally!"

My brow furrowed; eyes narrowed. Was it all a test? Had she been teaching me a lesson all my life? The beatings, scars, fear; was it all for this moment?

"You did it, Hansel. Now you can truly become one of God's soldiers." She sighed. "I can finally retire."

"Retire? From what?" She didn't work. Not many women worked in the lace factory around here.

"From saving souls. It's your turn now."

There was a knock at the door. Mama sat down, nursing her hand. I went to open it. Barbara was there. "What on earth happened to you?" she asked.

"I, my Mama," I said.

"Why?"

"I stood up for myself Barbara."

She smiled. "You did?" Her eyes widened and she grinned. "Is she still alive?" The fact that she said this made my jaw drop. Did she know what I was capable of? I nodded. "Come on, you need to get that cleaned up. Who knows what was on the knife before she used it?"

"Hmm, good point!" I followed her in the kitchen, unafraid of Mama seeing Barbara anymore. She said she'd retired after all. But what did she mean, it's my turn? Am I the one who needs to save souls now?

"What are you thinking?" Barbara said, passing me a clean cloth. I cleaned up my face, and it hurt. It hurt. Maybe I was starting to feel for once!

"My Mama said something strange."

"I heard her when I was outside. Thought it best to wait."

"You heard her! What did you hear?"

"That it's your turn, Hansel. You need to save the souls of the damned."

"So, you know what my Mama did?"

"Yes, she is holy and an inspiration to me and my family."

"But what about the grief she's caused."

"Grief is needed for people to heal. But don't worry Hansel, God always has a plan. It's your turn now."

A harsh voice yelled from the front room. "What are you doing Hansel?" Mama yelled.

I winced, if she came in, she would see Barbara. Taking a deep breath, I decided I had to face this straight on. But before I could, there was another knock at the door. Barbara nodded, pushing me to answer it.

"Get the door, Hansel!" Mama yelled.

Opening up I saw Lola Jane before me, looking past me into my home.

"Who is it?" Mama yelled.

Lola smiled. "Hi Hansel, you weren't at the swings this morning." She looked up. "What happened to your face?" she asked, eyes wide.

"It's nothing," I said.

"Invite her in," Barbara said.

"Hansel answer me! Who is it?" Mama yelled; her voice harsher than before.

"It's a friend from the park Mama, nothing to worry about."

"Boy or girl?" she asked, an air of curiosity in her voice.

Lola smiled. "Hi," she yelled. "I'm Lola."

Mama arrived behind me, staring down at Lola. "Oh, come in, come in." She grinned.

Lola nodded, walking past me. I was still holding the door open. Why was Mama acting so nice?

Following them into the front room, I stood behind Lola, and she sat down in the armchair. Barbara stood beside me. "So, Lola, what side of town are you from?"

"The south side Mam."

"Near the cliffs?"

"Yes, Mam."

Mama's brow wrinkled. "And what does your father do for work?"

"My father left Mam, it's just me and my Mama."

"Hmm, then how does your Mama support you?"

"I don't know Mam; she goes out a lot at night."

Mama's eyes bulged and she took a quick inhale of breath. Glaring at me she said, "Hansel, show her the tunnels. She will like it there."

"Why Mama?" I asked. Was she thinking what I was thinking? Surely, she can't believe this girl's mother worked the streets at night. Mama growled as she stood up. Lola's face paled. I stood there, unsure what to do.

Looking at Barbara she shrugged. "It's your turn now," she said, pushing me forward. Did she want to see me kill this girl?

Mama walked forward; she looked as angry as a demon spawned from Hell. Grabbing Lola's thin arm, she dragged her downstairs towards the tunnels.

"I have a present down there for you Hansel," she said, holding a wriggling Lola. "I had it bought in ready for you. You just need to finish it." She grinned.

"A present?" I frowned.

"Go see it and take this poor excuse for a girl with you!" She shoved Lola towards me.

I nodded and took a deep breath. There was no way of getting out of this one.

Downstairs I stomped through the tunnels. Barbara ran in front gushing as she saw my Mamas present. "Look Hansel," she said as I turned the corner and saw it. My eyes lit up. Mama was right, now I was ready to be a soldier of God.

Mama caught up, standing beside me. The screams of Lola Jane hurt my ears. I shoved her to the side, and she fell, smashing her head on the moss-covered stone wall.

All was quiet again. I sighed, relief taking over.

Right before me was the largest cage I'd ever seen. It covered the span of the room. Turning this end of the tunnel into a work of art. Shiny steel embedded into the stonework. A large, locked door sat in the middle; and two makeshift beds stood at the far end.

I was speechless!

"Do you like it?" she said.

I nodded. "Good. It just needs tightening up in areas, then it's all yours. You said you wanted the chance to see if you could heal them. Well, I conversed with our lord, and he came to me in a dream."

My jaw dropped. "You saw him?"

"I saw his light shining on this cage Hansel."

My eyes bulged. "So, he wants this… for me?"

"Yes. He wants you to give each girl a chance Hansel. Take them and if you can cure them, then they stand a better chance of walking through the gates of Heaven."

I nodded. It makes sense. To kill them as they were, would give them no time to repent for their sins, or the sins of their family.

Mama walked over and looked down at Lola. "It looks like she's already dead."

"I'd say so!" Barbara said, almost laughing. "She's lying in a pool of blood!"

I smiled, turning towards Barbara. "I know. But will you help me choose them?" she nodded. "Good, then Mama can retire."

Mama looked at me, her eyes narrowed. "Who on Earth are you talking to Hansel?" she said, confused.

I stepped back, staring at Barbara. What was she on about? "I think she's found out," she said.

"Found out what?"

"Hansel! Answer me!"

"Found out about us Hansel. Remember it's you and I forevermore."

I smiled, walked towards her, and held her body close to mine.

"Hansel, what are you doing?"

I shook my head. "Can't you see Mama, Barbara's going to help me!"

"Who's Barbara Hansel? There's no one there!"

I half laughed, "She's right here Mama, can't you see me holding her?"

She laughed, her cackles echoing in the tunnels.

"You're crazy Hansel. There's no one there."

I let go of Barbara. She looked at me with tearful eyes.

Anger raged through me. "Stop Mama!" I said. "You're upsetting her!"

She stopped laughing. Her brow furrowed. "You see her, don't you?"

I nodded. "Of course I do!"

Her face reddened, her hands fisted and her back straightened. She opened the cage door, pushed me backwards and toppled over landing on the concrete. "You and your demon can go in there!" she yelled, slamming the cage door shut, and locking us in.

"Wait!" I yelled, grabbing at the bars. Barbara began to cry.

"You're not ready Hansel! You must kill your demon first!"

"What?"

"No!" Barbara yelled. "I'm not a demon! I'm Hansel's friend!" She fell to the floor, her body phasing in and out of reality. What was happening? This couldn't be real! Where was she going? My Barbara had been with me for years, she'd soothed me when I was upset, laughed with me, and kissed me. It was all real! Barbara was real!

I knelt beside her, trying to take her hand. Matter dispersed. Skin disappeared.

"Barbara?" I said, totally confused.

"I'm fading Hansel! Help me!"

"What's happening?" I said, scared for her.

"Don't you remember Hansel? Don't you remember me?"

"Of course, I remember you!" I said, shouting at her now.

Mama shook her head and stormed off, back down the tunnel.

"She killed me, Hansel. She killed me for holding your hand."

"What?" I asked. "How can that be?"

"You must remember!" she yelled, staring at her phasing hands.

"I, I can't! I don't want to!"

"You must! Think back, Hansel. Remember when we were eight."

"Eight?"

"The Hollow, Hansel. You took me to the Hollow."

I thought back to the young girl beside the woods. The beautiful girl. My one true friend. I couldn't remember her name, but I did remember her hair, shiny long brown hair, as it blew in the wind, curling over her face. Those delicate pale hands when she moved it away from her eyes. Soft, smooth skin. Vibrant blue eyes. She looked at me, and our eyes met, just as our eyes were meeting right now. Could it be? Could my lifelong friend be the child my Mama strangled?

"Barbara?" I asked. She nodded, tears streaming from her eyes. "Are you real," I asked. She shook her head, her lips quivering.

"You needed me, Hansel."

"I still do Barbara, don't leave me!" I reached out, trying to clasp her hand in mine.

"I don't want to Hansel. I want to stay beside you forevermore."

"Then stay Barbara, help me to help them."

She nodded, wiping her eyes. Staring down at her hands, she began to smile. Skin phased back to reality. Pale features caressed her body once more. The girl I knew, my best friend and lifelong companion was coming back to me once again.

I smiled, taking her hand. As our skin touched, she whimpered. I held on tight, pulling her towards me, our bodies colliding. Holding her, I never wanted to let go, and if it meant I would remain caged for my whole life, then so be it. Barbara may not be real to others, but to me, she was everything, and no matter what I would never let my Mama take her from me.

12

Days turned to weeks. Weeks to years. Mama came and fed me daily, emptied the bucket and threw in the odd book or magazine. It was hard to keep up with the world outside, but I didn't mind. I had my Barbara, and to be honest, the cage was now my home.

Every time Mama opened the door, she would leave it ajar, I never left. These tunnels were the only life I knew.

Eventually, Barbara talked me into pulling my bed to another section of the tunnels. She stayed with me every step and helped me walk through, and feel my new surroundings. Mama still came, even though her legs weren't what they used to be. Doors were left open, and bones were thrown down from victims she had taken. I built a shrine for them in my room, a way of remembering their spirits, hoping they had the chance to walk through the pearl gates and sit before God.

"It's now or never," Barbara would say, holding my hand and helping me up the stairs. Light bled into my eyes; pain ignited within me. The world had changed above, become something I no longer knew or cared for. But I had a job to do, and as Mama could no longer fight to save their souls, I knew it was my turn. And so, at forty years of age, I walked the streets of Hilltop Meadows, spied on my neighbours, and listened in to absurd conversations. There were just too many souls that needed saving. Then I saw her, a sweet girl only eight years old. She reminded me so much of Barbara at that age. The living, full-bodied Barbara. Barbara clapped her hands, excitement caressed her features, and we went to work, taking our first caged soul, our first child, our Jess.

The End.

Continue with Red, the third book in the Gruesome Fairytales series.

OTHER BOOKS BY ANNALEE

Gretel

Hansel

Red

AUTHOR'S NOTE

Thank you for reading Hansel, I hope you enjoyed the story! I always appreciate your feedback and would be grateful if you could leave me a review on Amazon– just a few words make all the difference!

As with all authors, reviews mean the world to me. It keeps me going, helps me strengthen my writing style and helps this story become a success. If you enjoyed reading Hansel, and have already read Gretel, then the next in the series Red is based on Red Riding Hood, and tells the tale of murder, revenge and vigilante justice.

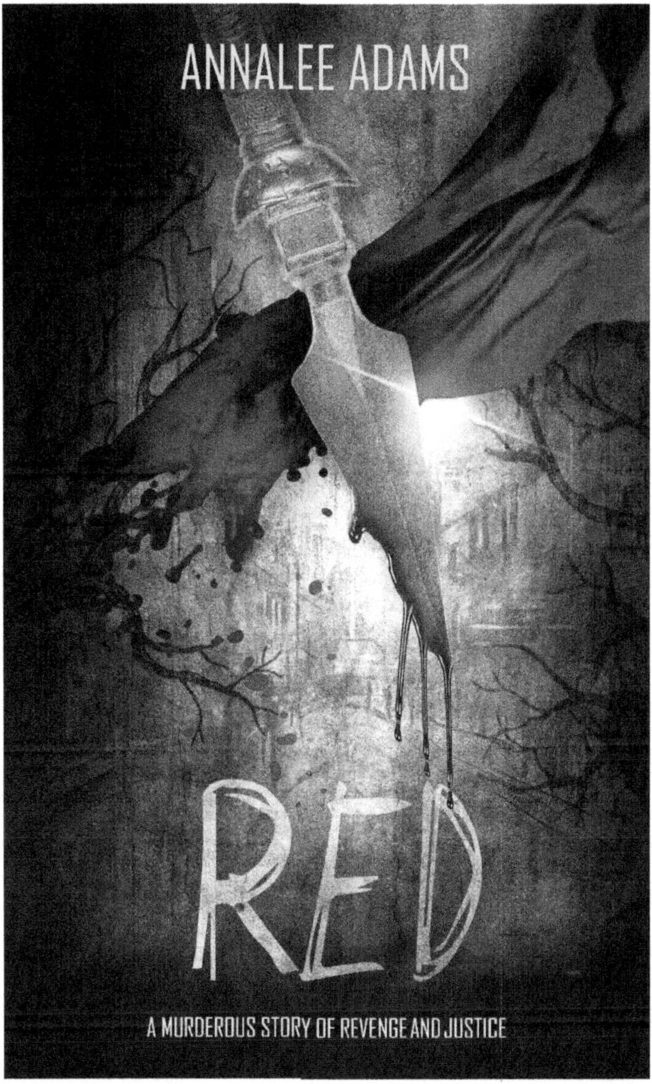
ANNALEE ADAMS
RED
A MURDEROUS STORY OF REVENGE AND JUSTICE

CONNECT WITH ANNALEE

Join Annalee on social media. She is regularly posting videos and updates for her next books on TikTok and Facebook.

Join Annalee in her Facebook group:

Annalee Adams Bookworms & Bibliophiles.

Also, subscribe to Annalee's newsletter through her website - for free books, sales, sneak previews and much more.

Subscribe at www.AnnaleeAdams.biz

TikTok: @author_annaleeadams

Website: www.AnnaleeAdams.biz

Email: AuthorAnnaleeAdams@gmail.com

Facebook:

https://www.facebook.com/authorannaleeadams/

ABOUT ANNALEE

Annalee Adams was born in Ashby de la Zouch, England. Annalee spent much of her childhood engrossed in fictional stories, starting with teenage point horror stories and moving on to the works of Stephen King and Dean Koontz. However, her all-time favourite book is Lewis Carroll's, Alice in Wonderland.

Annalee lives in the UK with her husband, two fantastic children, little dog Milo, and cat Luna. She's a lover of long walks on the beach, strong cups of tea and reading a good book.

Printed in Great Britain
by Amazon

42867722R00061